SCOTT STARKEY

THE CALL of the BULLY

A Rodney Rathbone Novel

A PAULA WISEMAN BOOK
Simon & Schuster Books for Young Readers
New York London Toronto Sydney New Delhi

ALSO BY SCOTT STARKEY

How to Beat the Bully Without Really Trying

SIMON & SCHUSTER BOOKS FOR YOUNG READERS
An imprint of Simon & Schuster Children's Publishing Division
1230 Avenue of the Americas, New York, New York 10020
This book is a work of fiction. Any references to historical
events, real people, or real places are used fictitiously. Other names, characters, places,
and events are products of the author's imagination, and any resemblance to
actual events or places or persons, living or dead, is entirely coincidental.
Copyright © 2013 by Scott Starkey
Cover illustration copyright © 2013 by Tim Jessell
All rights reserved, including the right of reproduction in whole or in part in any form.
SIMON & SCHUSTER BOOKS FOR YOUNG READERS is a trademark of Simon & Schuster, Inc.
For information about special discounts for bulk purchases, please contact Simon &
Schuster Special Sales at 1-866-506-1949 or business@simonandschuster.com.
The Simon & Schuster Speakers Bureau can bring authors to your live event.
For more information or to book an event, contact the Simon & Schuster Speakers
Bureau at 1-866-248-3049 or visit our website at www.simonspeakers.com.
Also available in a Simon & Schuster Books for Young Readers hardcover edition
Book design by Krista Vossen
The text for this book is set in Bembo Std.
Manufactured in the United States of America
0414 OFF
First Simon & Schuster Books for Young Readers paperback edition January 2014
2 4 6 8 10 9 7 5 3
The Library of Congress has cataloged the hardcover edition as follows:
Starkey, Scott.
The call of the bully : a Rodney Rathbone novel / Scott Starkey.
p. cm
Summary: Stuck at Camp Wy-Mee, cowardly Rodney Rathbone is forced to try
to make friends and finds himself once again in the unlikely roll of camp hero.
ISBN 978-1-4424-5674-7 (hc)
[1. Camps—Fiction. 2. Bullies—Fiction. 3. Friendship—Fiction. 4. Humorous stories.]
I. Title.
PZ7.S7952Cal 2013
[Fic]—dc23
2012039444
ISBN 978-1-4424-5675-4 (pbk)
ISBN 978-1-4424-5676-1 (eBook)

Dedicated to my daughter, Brooke

Acknowledgments

Most authors have people who help them along the way and I am no exception. Once again, I thank Paula Wiseman and everyone else at Simon & Schuster for their belief in me. I thank my wife, Judy, for all her support, ideas, and for helping me find time in our busy schedules to write. I also thank all the kids out there who enjoyed Rodney's first adventure. Your letters keep me very motivated!

Lastly, I want to thank my friend Lloyd Singer. It was his encouragement that got me writing years ago, his criticism that made me a stronger writer, and his edits that helped make this a book I'm very proud to share with you.

CONTENTS

Chapter 1

THE VAN RIDE

Through the van window I watched Mrs. Lutzkraut shake my dad's hand and give my mom a big hug. Then she turned to wave good-bye to me. On her face was a smile—a perfectly evil grin. I'd never seen her look so happy. My demented former teacher and I shared a secret, you see. I was about to die, and she knew it.

The cause of my inevitable end, Josh, was on the van with me. And as my parents and Mrs. Lutzkraut disappeared in the distance, I shifted my eyes to watch him. He sat across the aisle, glaring out the window. There was one other kid in the back of the van, but he had been asleep when Josh and I climbed on. I doubted he would come to my rescue when Josh attacked.

An old, familiar feeling of terror began to rise from my stomach. There was no doubt in my mind that Josh was about to crush me. I mean, that had been his main goal the entire school year. Now all that separated us was about six feet. I rubbed my sweaty palms on my shorts and stared out the window.

Maybe Josh would wait until we got to summer camp before killing me. That meant I had about two hours left to enjoy life. Only there was nothing to enjoy and nothing happy to think about. I was being shipped off to someplace called Camp Wy-Mee with my worst enemy. For eight weeks!

Oh yes, Mrs. Lutzkraut had a lot to be smiling about this afternoon. She had tricked my parents—and Josh's parents—into thinking summer camp was the best thing in the world. Josh hadn't looked too pleased about it either. I shifted in the uncomfortable van seat and let my eyes wander in his direction. Big mistake.

"Forget about me, Rathbone?"

He must have been staring at me the whole time. This was it. I tried to answer but nothing came out.

"Yeah, Rathbone, you ain't that tough. I could see you were real scared at graduation. I was a fool all year, thinkin' you were tough. This time nothing's saving you. Punching you's gonna be like Christmas morning. Guess that makes me Santa."

I didn't understand his logic, but I understood what it meant when his legs shifted into the aisle. I raised my arms in a feeble attempt to block the incoming buffalo stampede.

Vroom! The engine revved and I could feel tires skidding on sand. The van swerved, knocking Josh off-balance. I watched as Santa banged his head on the floor.

"You there!" the driver hollered.

"Me?" I squeaked.

"Yeah, you." I could see the driver's grizzled face and dark eyes in the big rearview mirror. "Help that kid up." Josh was rolling around in the aisle, dazed and holding his head. "Go on, put him in a seat."

I looked closer at the driver. He wore a ripped tank top and had a big bushy beard. "Do I have to?" I asked.

"Do it!" the driver ordered.

I reached down to grab Josh under the arms just as the driver turned his attention back to the road. The van swerved violently, knocking *me* off-balance. I landed with a crunch, right on top of Josh.

"No more, no more," he whimpered. "I'll behave, Rodney, I promise. Just leave me alone."

I backed away and watched him climb into his seat, where he curled up into a ball. My jaw hung low, shocked. There was no tougher kid than Josh. He was like twice my size. Thanks to the van driver's horrible driving, Josh had been knocked down before he could even throw a punch. Maybe my amazing run of luck from the school year wasn't over. Not just yet, anyway.

Chapter 2

MY NEW BEAST FRIEND

Josh had been quiet for about an hour as we drove along—probably wondering how I always got the best of him. "You look pretty runty," he finally muttered. "I don't get it. How come you fight good?"

"Well," I corrected him. My mom's constant grammar reminders were rubbing off on me.

"Huh?"

"How come you fight *well*."

"Oh, I guess because I'm tough." I rolled my eyes. He continued, "But how come you fight good too, Rathbone?"

He was still holding the side of his head. I relaxed a little and my big mouth kicked into gear. "For starters, I have natural killer instincts. Combine that with years of high-intensity combat training, not to mention . . ."

He was looking at me intently now, but I'm not sure how much was reaching his brain. Finally he just smiled and said, "Yeah, fighting's good."

It was the first time I'd ever seen him smile, not counting when he inflicted pain on some poor kid. He turned and looked out the window for a moment. "You know," he continued, "I beat up over a hundred kids and never lost one fight. Then you beat me up two times. Plus today. That makes . . ."

The higher math was too much for him. "Three," I informed him.

"Yeah, whatever. It's just, I still can't believe it." He sounded both disappointed and respectful. "Before you came along I did whatever I wanted, took whatever I wanted, beat up whoever I wanted, did whatever I wanted . . ."

I couldn't believe we were having a conversation. A weird, creepy conversation, but a conversation. Usually he just grunted or told me how he was going to knock my face apart. "I never wanted to ruin your year," I explained, "but you're the one who picked a fight. You play with fire, you get burned."

"You like fire, too?"

Boy, this kid was thick. "Yeah, fire's pretty cool," I agreed. I was willing to play along if it meant keeping his hands off my neck.

"I love fire! I got a lighter. You want to help me light this seat on fire?"

"I think we should probably leave the seats alone. You see," I explained, "we're traveling in the van that you want to set fire to."

He seemed to contemplate that for a minute.

"Anyway, Rathbone, you're actually not that bad. Hey, check this out." With a dumb grin etched on his lips, he began punching the back of the seat in front of him. I, on the other hand, wrestled with the vision of bunk beds burning in my cabin.

I gazed out the window and watched the Ohio countryside pass by, each mile taking me farther from home. I was miserable. Sure, I had dodged a bullet with Josh, but you have to understand the incredible school year that was still fresh in my mind. When it started, I was the new kid in town, afraid of getting pounded to a pulp at school. Then, through pure luck, I became Mr. Popular. Hero of the Town. Czar of the Playground! I met Rishi, Slim, and Dave—the three best friends I'd ever had. No group could make me laugh so hard. Rishi was the big talker and had outlined a million awesome things for us to do this summer. None of it would be happening now—with me, at least.

As the van zoomed down the highway I thought about something else that was making me miserable. I had left behind my girlfriend, Jessica. We'd been "officially" going out for about twenty minutes when my parents dropped the camp bomb.

"Hey, Rodney," Josh suddenly called out from his seat.

Whatever he was about to say, no matter how dumb, I actually welcomed the distraction. Anything to get my mind off Jessica! "Yeah?" I asked.

"You going out with Jessica?"

Evidently I was traveling with the Amazing Moron Mind Reader. "I don't want to talk about it," I answered.

"Uh, okay, so you going out with her?"

His words hurt more than his fists ever could. I didn't know if being apart from her was going to end our relationship. I sighed. "Listen, she's not happy with me going away and all."

"No? Don't feel bad, though."

"Why not?" I asked.

"Because she's real pretty. She'll find a new boyfriend in no time."

I stared at the gorilla sitting next to me. "How's that supposed to make me feel better?"

"Huh? Oh, I guess I got that backward. Yeah, you should feel bad. Hey, driver, I gotta take a whiz!"

I watched the driver's face in the rearview mirror. He was chewing on a toothpick. "We'll be at camp soon."

He had introduced himself as . . . hmm, was it Grizzly Bob, or Creepy Bill, or Smelly Stan? . . . No, it was Survival Steve. He had a bushy beard and a deep voice, and his eyes were dark and menacing. Worst of all, he wore a big hunting knife on his leather belt.

Josh didn't seem to notice or care. "I gotta go so bad I could fill a pool!"

Survival Steve's eyebrows rose for a moment. "We'll take a shortcut, down the old logger road. You can go on the side somewhere. It'll save time and it's good scenery." He banked down the next exit ramp off the highway, turned left, and eventually made a right on a dirt road.

I'm not sure you could really call it a road. After a while the trees and branches closed in and began whacking the sides of the van. Josh's face was scrunched up and he was holding himself. I moved farther away, not wanting to get sprayed by a yellow geyser. "Pull over!" he yelled.

Survival Steve said, "Hold your water. That looks like a good spot up ahead." He brought the van to a stop. "Guess you can go . . ."

Josh didn't wait. He bolted out the door and off into the woods.

"All right, how about you two?"

I needed to go, though probably not as badly as Josh. I could hear him moaning off in the woods. As I angled toward the door I noticed that the kid in the back was awake now. He shook his head, and his eyes looked frightened under the brim of his red baseball cap. I couldn't blame him for being nervous, considering we were stopped in the middle of nowhere. After glancing around, he curled up and pulled his hat down further.

I climbed out and walked a few paces away from the van into the woods. The dark pine forest smelled thick and sweet, and the air hung heavy. It was real quiet and eerie. I noticed that the sun was already setting behind the tallest trees. As I finished my business, I shivered and realized I couldn't wait to get back in the van.

"Beautiful, ain't it?" It was Survival Steve.

"I guess," I answered.

"Yup, these woods are something special. I once lived in them by myself for three years. Killed a moose with only a rock, like this one. Moose liver, now that's tasty stuff."

I looked back at him. The word *insane* flashed through my mind.

"What's your name?" he asked.

"Rodney."

"Rodney, check this out!" He picked up the rock and flung it right at a tree. A huge section of bark shattered from the trunk. "Aim still perfect." He grinned. "Nothing beats a good stone." I was too scared to comment. "Rodney, you come by my shack at camp, I'll teach you to throw a stone like that, better yet I'll show you how to use a bow and arrow."

Avoid all shacks this summer, I thought as we returned to the van.

"You!" Steve hollered at Josh, who was back from the woods. "Go get that other kid and see if he wants a soda."

Josh made an evil grin and I knew what was coming as he climbed inside the van. The next sound I heard would be . . .

Thwack!

"Owwwww!" screamed the unsuspecting kid. "Why'd you hit me?"

"Driver said to," Josh declared.

"Huh?"

Whack!

"Owwwww!"

The poor kid tumbled out of the van. "Where the heck are we?" he asked, moving away from Josh, who had jumped down behind him. Survival Steve stepped forward, rock in hand. The kid's lips started quivering as he backed away, a look of panic building on his face.

"Guess I'll open this sucker up with Old Reliable," Survivor Steve announced. The rock raised, ready to strike.

"Whooaahhhh!" The kid was off like a shot, tearing into the woods.

"I was only talking about this can of soda," Steve laughed. "The opener thing broke. Now I gotta go get that scaredy-cat. You two, wait here."

I suddenly found myself alone with Josh in the middle of nowhere. Thank God we had "bonded" on the van, because instead of threatening me like he'd done in the past, he told me a story about a time he had punched his friend Toby in the face at school. We were both laughing when Survival Steve came trudging back from the woods.

"All right, we got problems. That kid ran off. Far. We're all going to have to go find him. We better spread out because we don't want to be out here in the dark."

All too familiar feelings began to creep along my spine. I looked nervously into the woods. The trees were thick, blocking out most of the light. "We're going in *there*?" I croaked.

"Yup. You, big fella, head off to my right. And you," he said, eyeing me, "you walk in on my left. Use the sun to navigate."

Sun to navigate? I grew up in Queens, in New York City. Only navigating I could do was hailing a cab.

"Let's go," he barked. I walked so close to him that if I'd gotten any closer he'd be giving me a piggyback ride. "What the . . . ? Spread out. Go to the left! We can't find him all bunched up, and we don't want to be out here when it gets dark."

It took great courage on my part to move into the woods on my own. In less than five minutes the courage ran out. Steve was nowhere in sight. *Well, I'll just head back to the van*, I told myself. I turned around and started walking, but with each step my heart beat a little faster. Nothing looked familiar. Sweat poured down into my eyes. As I caught my breath, my brain whispered two little words that didn't exactly calm me. *You're lost.*

"Help!!!" I screamed. "Joshhhh!!! Crazy driverrrr!!!" Maybe that was a mistake. "Anybody!!! Help!!!"

I heard my echo, then silence. I tried again a few more times before my voice began to give out.

I sat down on a big rock. *Someone will find you*, I

lied to myself. I thought about my parents and my little sister back in Garrettsville. I thought about my friends and wondered what they were up to. Then my thoughts turned to Jessica. Only yesterday I had told her about going away to camp.

"Rodney, why didn't you tell me sooner?" she had asked.

"I didn't know," I explained. "My dopey dad surprised me after the graduation ceremony."

"Well, what about us? What about the lake and the pool and . . ."

"Ugh, I know! I can't get out of it. I've tried. I won't be gone forever."

"How long?"

"Eight weeks."

"Eight weeks? That *is* forever. It's longer. It's the whole summer!"

I tried to calm her. "We'll be going to middle school together in the fall. I'll write you."

"I guess you can always call while you're away, or text . . ."

"Actually, we're not allowed to have cell phones." The words had hung there as she realized we weren't even going to speak. She looked really upset, making my heart sink low into my stomach. It felt the same now, sitting on this rock in the woods.

Sitting on this rock in the woods? I had lost total track of time! It was almost dark now. *Think. What would*

Survival Steve do? Besides killing a moose, he'd probably get something to protect himself. Yes, that's it.

I looked around and found a big stick. I felt better clutching it and headed off in what I hoped was the direction of the van. Just when it was getting so dark I could barely see, I noticed something red up ahead—the baseball cap of the kid who had run off.

"Hey!" I yelled. "Found you!"

He turned around, saw me, and tore off.

"Wait!" I shouted, running after him. There was no way I was going to let this kid leave me alone in the woods. "Stop!" I shouted. The kid looked back, screamed, and kept going. Why was he running away? "Stop running! Get back here," I yelled, my own fear building up again.

After about five minutes of running through thick underbrush and sharp branches—my legs were scratched all over—I noticed a bright glow up ahead. The kid was running toward it. I followed, gaining on him. We were going to be saved!

He bolted through a bush and I dove through too, landing right in the middle of a large crowd of kids, some wearing Camp Wy-Mee T-shirts. The light was from a roaring campfire! I was about to yell, "Thank God, I'm saved," but old Baseball Cap beat me to it.

"Oh, thank God!" he screamed, his voice higher than I expected. "That madman was chasing me through the woods." He pointed at me. "They tried to kill me back at the van!" The kid was gasping for air and looked on the verge of collapse.

My brain reeled with every emotion as I realized I had just gone from saved to public enemy number one. I glanced around at the crowd. No one knew what to make of me as I stood there in my ripped, sweaty, dirty clothes. Their looks ranged from fearful to suspicious to menacing. I glanced at my hand, holding the stick that suddenly resembled a club. "Yikes," I gulped, dropping it with a quick jerk. This was bad. "Wait," I stammered, "it's not what you think . . ."

My mouth, however, couldn't complete the sentence, for at that moment the kid flung off his baseball cap. Long brown hair tumbled down past his shoulders. I mean, *her* shoulders. It was a girl standing there, with emerald green eyes that flashed in the firelight. Even in the middle of the insane moment I could see she was cute. *Real* cute. If I didn't get burned at the stake, summer camp had just gotten a lot more interesting.

Chapter 3

THE FIRE FIGHT

There was a pause as everyone stared at the girl. I guess at first they thought she was a boy, too, but there was no mistaking her now. I started to back away, knowing it was only a matter of seconds before the campfire crowd remembered the madman in their midst.

"This guy tried to kill you?" one boy asked. He was taller than me but looked about my age. Before the girl could answer, he faced the group and ordered, "Grab him!"

Two older teenagers came forward and held me by the arms. The boy giving orders walked up to me as I struggled to break free. Even in the dark I could see he had a white, toothy smile. He flicked his hair to the side like a shampoo model. "Trying to get away?" He laughed. "Not today, weirdo." He gave me a little wink and raised his fist to punch me.

I had never been so scared, which is quite a claim,

considering who I am. Without thinking, though, I lunged forward. The two guys holding my arms banged into the boy, sending him flying backward—right into the fire.

"Oh, Todd!" some girl called out.

Todd screeched, "*Yaaaaaahhhhhhhhhhhooooooooh!*" and jumped up, grabbing his behind.

"The lake!" the girl yelled.

I watched Todd run off into the woods, leaving a smoke trail from his scorched shorts. The guys holding me grabbed even tighter.

I was just starting to ponder my funeral—I pictured Mrs. Lutzkraut smiling happily—when Josh and Survival Steve emerged from the woods. "You got started without me, Rodney!" Josh shouted while grabbing a kid and hurling him over a log. "Fire and fighting. This is awesome. I love camp!"

Survival Steve looked at the guys holding me. "What you fools doin'? Let my passenger be! Josh, settle down."

My captors released me from their grip. At the same moment, Todd returned, his pants dripping wet. He took one look at Survival Steve and sneered. "We got it under control, Mountain Man. You can head back to your shack now."

"What's that, punk?"

"The name's Todd."

"Yeah, I remember you, Turd. Now git!" Steve roared like a grizzly bear and Todd scuttled off into the crowd around the campfire. Next he shouted, "Periwinkle, you down here?"

"Yes," a large tree replied.

Steve glanced about for a second. Not sure where to look, he called out, "These two are with me. I was bringing them in when we had to go in search of another camper."

"Ohhh," the tree answered. Then, slowly, from behind the tree, a head wearing an odd beige pith helmet popped out. Eventually, the rest of the man emerged, and the guy I assumed to be Mr. Periwinkle now stood in the firelight. His outfit matched his helmet. It was all khaki and he looked like an explorer—a skinny, jumpy, nervous explorer.

"Okay then," he finally spoke, eyes darting nervously to make sure the fighting was over. "This looks like a big misunderstanding. Welcome to Camp Wy-Mee! Nice to meet you two, and you, young lady." He waved to the girl.

"She's not with us," Steve pointed out.

"Uh, actually she is," I corrected him. "It's a long story."

Steve glanced at the girl, then at me, then back at the girl. A smile slowly broke across his puzzled face. "Well, I'll be a skinned possum . . ."

"Um, yes, a possum," Mr. Periwinkle continued. "As I was saying, this is the opening night campfire. It's usually a very exciting, fun tradition. Oh, well, I guess it was still exciting. Ha-ha." His laugh sure was nervous. With a strained face, he asked, "Are either of you hurt?" I shook my head and heard him murmur, "Thank God, no lawsuits."

Josh, who had never stopped grinning since he got to camp, explained, "We don't mess around."

"Yes, well, you're quite a strapping fellow," Mr. Periwinkle remarked. "So you're not hurt either, good. No need to call the parents, ha-ha-ha." Again the nervous laugh. "Okay, I guess this is enough campfire for one evening. Counselors, take your campers back to the cabins and prepare for taps. You, douse that fire. And you, move that log . . ."

He continued giving nervous little orders. I was relieved that the threat of violence had passed, at least for now, but this Mr. Periwinkle had said something about calling the parents, and that's exactly what I intended to do first thing in the morning. All I had to do right now was survive the rest of the night.

Chapter 4

A NIGHT AT THE PLAZA

Without the campfire, the air suddenly got colder and the woods grew a lot darker. I looked up through the tall pine trees and noticed a few stars beginning to come out. Mr. Periwinkle was chattering away to the remaining counselors. No one seemed to notice me—except Todd, the kid I had just knocked into the fire. Every few seconds he would shine his flashlight in my eyes to annoy me. It was definitely working.

Turning in my direction, Mr. Periwinkle called over, "You're still standing here?" He said it in a nice enough way.

"I don't know where to go."

"I guess that's a good reason, then." He laughed nervously. "You *did* arrive after the cabin assignments. Let's consult the clipboard." He picked up the board and shuffled through the sheets. "Let me see. Hmmm . . . Rathbone, right?"

"Yes."

"Hmmmm, Rathbone, Rathbone . . . Ah, there we go. Well now, aren't *you* the lucky little camper?"

Was this guy for real? My fellow campers were just about to roast me like a marshmallow. Somehow I didn't feel too lucky.

Periwinkle kept right on beaming. "Yes, you are in for quite a treat. You, my son, have been assigned to the Algonquin cabin."

The name meant little to me. As if reading my mind, he explained that the Algonquins were a Native American tribe. He went on and on about how they carried tomahawks and hunted with bows and arrows in woods just like these. After a minute he stopped midsentence, looking slightly confused. "Where was I? Oh yes, let me find someone to show you the way to the cabin."

As Mr. Periwinkle turned, Todd started in again with the flashlight in my eyes. I was beginning to wish I had a tomahawk of my own when Mr. Periwinkle called out to him. He immediately pointed the light to the ground. "Yes?"

"Please come over here and join us, Todd."

This was the last kid I wanted to give me a welcome tour—or to be my roommate, which was even worse. I had to speak up. "Mr. Periwinkle, isn't there another cabin I could . . ."

"I wouldn't hear of it. Rodney, let me introduce you to Todd Vanderdick. Todd, this is Rodney Rathbone."

The two of us stared at each other, neither one wanting to make the first move. Periwinkle shot nervous glances back and forth between us. His eyes seemed to ask, *Well?* Reluctantly, we shook hands. As they came together, I could feel my skin crawl.

"That's a clammy palm you got there," Todd said, sticking out his big chin.

"Not as clammy as your pants," I answered. "Enjoy the dip in the lake?"

Mr. Periwinkle glanced down. "I say, Todd, what happened to your shorts?"

Todd's eyes narrowed and a sneer curled over his perfect, gleaming teeth. "My hand-tailored $225 Lacoste shorts? I doubt the rodent who ruined them could afford to buy me new ones, but no matter—I have twelve more pairs just like them."

"Excellent," Mr. Periwinkle exclaimed. "It's wise to come prepared. Now, I can see that the two of you are going to be fast friends. Rodney here is in your cabin. I thought you'd like to show him around and introduce him to the boys."

Todd's chin quivered and it looked as though he was trying to eat his own lip. After about ten seconds he became oddly relaxed and his face transformed into an easy smile. The transformation gave me a nervous feeling. With sparkling eyes, he announced, "It would be my pleasure, Mr. Periwinkle."

"Splendid."

Todd held up his finger. "One more thing. What happened to Rodney's big friend?"

"I believe you're referring to young Dumbrowski. He's been assigned to the Cherokee cabin."

"That dump?" Todd laughed.

"Now, Todd, all our facilities here at Camp Wy-Mee can't be . . ."

"Oh, don't get me wrong, Mr. Periwinkle. I think Loserville is the perfect cabin for him, but I'm concerned about Rodney. After all, he'll be *really* far away from his friend. He's going to be all alone. I'll have to take *special* care of him."

"Todd, that's certainly noble of you. You see, Rodney? I leave you in good hands."

Mr. Periwinkle scurried away, and my nerves began firing every warning they knew. I almost collapsed when Todd suddenly gripped my shoulder. "Come on, old sport. Let me show you the way."

I shrugged off his grip as we meandered around trees and bushes. He angled down to a woods path that looked dark and foreboding. I gulped and hesitated. He seemed to sense it and turned back with a smile. "Don't fall behind, Rathbone. This isn't a stroll down Park Avenue. The last thing you want is to wind up lost out here."

He was acting awfully nice . . . for a jerk. Despite my suspicions, I didn't have much choice but to follow him.

★ ★ ★

Moments later we popped out onto a paved path, crossed some playing fields, and walked toward a group of cabins in the distance. I noticed the gleam from a number of flashlights shaking about in the dark. Other campers and counselors were also making the trek, which hopefully meant I wasn't about to get attacked.

"You're going to love the cabin," Todd said. "My dad, Theodore Vanderdick—you know, of *Vanderdick Enterprises*—donated money and his personal architect to spruce up the place."

I had never heard of Vanderdick Enterprises. "Sounds good," I managed.

"Oh, it's a lot better than 'good,' and certainly a lot better than the hole you just crawled out of. Yeah, your luck has turned, hasn't it, chap? Time to see how the other half lives." He spoke to me like I was homeless.

"You know," he continued, "I realize we got off to a bad start, but you have to admit you looked a bit crazy when you first showed up. And besides, now that you're on Team Vanderdick, it's time for a new beginning. What do you say, sport?"

I looked at him. My doubts lingered. He was definitely a stuck-up jerk, but maybe he wasn't out to get me. Maybe he *did* want to be friends. "Well, sorry about knocking you into the fire," I said. "It was an accident." I figured I'd better be nice since I was stuck in his cabin.

"Hey, accidents happen." He held out his hand.

I held out mine, hoping it wasn't clammy, and gave him my best Fred Windbagger handshake.

"That's the spirit," Todd said.

We walked up the path from the fields to a row of cabins. Most of them looked like little huts with some canvas flaps for windows. That is, until we came to a stop in front of one cabin that was three times larger than the rest. It had glass windows, a paved walkway and steps, and what looked like a satellite dish on the roof. I could hear the hum of central air conditioning. "It's not the Plaza, but it's home," Todd said, wiping his feet before pushing open the door.

He was being modest. I didn't think any hotel could be nicer. A group of boys sat around on leather couches, playing a video game on a gigantic flat-screen television that took up the whole wall.

"Hey, fellas, let me introduce to you to Rodney."

They paused the game. Their eyes narrowed and I prayed I wasn't about to get jumped. Some of them probably recognized me from the campfire.

Todd gripped my shoulder. "Rodney is assigned to the Algonquin cabin. Give him a big Team Vanderdick welcome."

The tension left their faces. In unison they chanted, "Bully! Bully! Bully!"

"Where?" I almost screamed, half expecting to see my old enemy, Rocco.

Todd laughed. "Relax, Rathbone. Let me introduce

you to everyone. This is Biff, Skip, Chaz, Blake, Chip"—
each gave me a friendly wave—"and over there, that's
our counselor, Magnus."

I turned. Standing behind a counter in the kitchen
area was a tall, strong-looking blond guy. I figured he was
about eighteen. "Velcome. Vat can I fix you to drink?"
he asked, shaking a silver cup up and down. "You vant
fruit smoothie?"

"Uh, sure."

"Rodney," Todd interrupted, "it looks like your
trunk's been dropped off. Maybe you want to put your
stuff away. What beds are still available?"

Biff answered, "The Tempur-Pedic and the Euro-
Flow 2000 waterbed." He looked kind of sheepish as he
added, "The good ones are taken already."

Todd glanced at me. "What do you think?"

"Both sound nice."

"Here's da smoothie," Magnus said, thrusting a cold
glass into my hand.

I took a sip and gagged as something slimy slid across
the top of my tongue. "Uh, delicious."

"I put in lots of raw egg. Goot for da muscles and da
hair." I was fighting the urge to heave and it must have
shown. "Vatch da Persian rug!"

Not sure I could survive another sip, I did my best
to be polite. "Is that a German accent?" I asked, putting
down the smoothie and pushing it a few inches away.

Magnus straightened up to his full height. "I am not

25

German!" He pounded his chest with his fist. "I am Sveeedish!"

He looked offended, so I said, "I love Sweden!"

"Really?" he asked.

"Oh yeah. Big fan of the meatballs."

"Dere's more to Sveden dan meatballs."

"No doubt," I agreed, struggling hard to think of something else. "Vikings!" I blurted. "I love Vikings."

Magnus smiled and I relaxed—until I noticed his expression start to change. He looked like he was about to cry. "Too bad vee are no longer allowed to raid and pillage. Nothing like dying vit da sword in your hands and going to Valhalla."

"Uh, yeah." The guy was definitely nuts. I looked over to Todd for help.

"Come on, Rodney. I'll show you around the cabin."

We left Magnus in the kitchen—hacking and slicing at the air as if he was raiding a monastery—and toured the rooms. All in all, it was more impressive than I could have imagined. They had every video game system, a pool table, a ping-pong table, a foosball table, and a very nice back deck overlooking the lake.

It was a hundred times better than my house at home!

Slowly, I began to realize that my teacher Mrs. Lutz-kraut had gotten me sent to paradise. I wished she could be here to see how her plan had backfired. I was now friends with Josh, this guy Todd seemed okay once you got to know him, and I'd be spending the summer in air-conditioned splendor. I sat down on the couch and folded my hands behind my head. Not bad. Not bad at all.

"There's only one thing we don't have," Todd apologized, "and that's our own bathroom. My dad's lawyers petitioned the head of the local zoning board for a year. When we didn't get our way, Vanderdick Enterprises built a massive prison next to the guy's summerhouse." A big grin spread across Todd's face. "What a loser. You don't mess with Vanderdick Enterprises, right, fellas?" Everyone in the cabin laughed in agreement. "Anyway, long story short, we have to use the boys' division bathroom with all the lowlifes. It's over there."

I looked out through the window. Even in the dark I thought I saw flies buzzing around the building. "Ugh."

Todd nodded. "Be thankful the breeze isn't blowing from the south. Nothing like the scent of old urine to spoil an evening." He stretched and yawned. "It's been a long night. We should turn in. Take the water bed, Rodney. Come on, guys, let's get some shut-eye."

And so for the next twenty minutes I settled in. Following a rather gross visit to the bathroom, I climbed into the water bed. I felt like I was lying on top of the waves. It was fun, and for the first time all day I let myself relax. Just as sleep began to take hold, I remember thinking how lucky I was to be in this cabin with my new friends. Yep, that old witch Lutzkraut had really miscalculated this time.

★ ★ ★

BLAM! BOOM! POP! BANG! I awoke to what sounded like gunfire. I rolled off the wavy bed to the floor and took cover. Yells and screams filled the night. The lights came on and my cabinmates rushed toward the door.

"What is it?"

Biff, who was gazing out the window, yelled, "There's smoke coming from the Loserville cabin!"

We tumbled out into the night. Counselors and campers were running all about. I considered heading back inside for safety but found myself swept along by the crew heading to Loserville.

Magnus boomed, "Voo! Voo!" I thought he'd really lost it until a tall Asian-looking counselor with long black hair stepped out of the smoke. Magnus ran up to him. "Voo, vat is going on?"

"His name is Voo?" I asked Biff, who was standing next to me.

"No, it's Woo."

Before I had a chance to ponder that I moved in closer to hear what Woo had to say.

"The night goes 'Pow!,' man. The campers yell 'Ow!,' man. Everyone's having a cow, man!"

It was confusing, to say the least, but Magnus seemed to understand perfectly. "Zumbody lit firevorks in da cabin!"

"That's certainly what it seems like," said Mr. Periwinkle, walking up to the crowd. I watched him pull his robe around what looked like animal-print pajamas.

"Who vould do dis?" Magnus bellowed, smashing his fist into his palm. "Deese campers could have been hurt."

I looked at the campers who inhabited Loserville. Several of them had smoke-smeared faces and were on the verge of tears. Josh stood off a bit, gazing at the smoke that remained hanging in the air.

"*I* know who did it," Todd suddenly announced. I wasn't expecting this.

"Who?" Magnus and Mr. Periwinkle asked together.

"He's standing right there."

I leaned my head in to see the culprit. What happened next was a complete shock. Todd pointed straight at me. "I'm very disappointed in you, Rathbone, though I can't say I'm surprised, given your upbringing."

"Huh?" I managed. Suddenly a sinking, sad feeling hit me in the gut as I realized what was about to happen. How could I have been so stupid? I had let myself believe that Todd really wanted to be my friend.

"I found these in Rodney's trunk," he lied, holding up several packs of fireworks. "His trunk was left open and I just happened to notice them. There's more where these came from."

"But I don't have any fireworks," I stammered. "I was asleep the whole night."

"Sure, Rathbone," he continued, "that's why I saw

you sneaking back from Loserville." His lips curled into a villainous leer and he gave me a subtle wink. No one else seemed to notice it, but I knew my excellent new buddy Todd had just framed me.

"Let's go and look in his trunk!" Magnus barked.

Todd wasn't finished. He grabbed the counselor's elbow. "Oh, we will, Magnus, but before I show you the proof of Rodney's guilt, I think we need to check on tonight's poor victims."

Where was he going with all this? I looked around at the crowd. Everyone was giving me nasty looks. Even Mr. Periwinkle seemed annoyed.

Todd walked over to the whimpering Loserville campers. "Are you guys okay?" he asked, giving one young boy a brotherly pat on the shoulder.

Mr. Periwinkle said, "You're right, Todd. I admire your compassion. We need to look into their well-being before we deal with Rodney."

Todd brought his hands to his heart. While he tried to look sincere, I caught a gleam in his eye that told me he wasn't finished plotting my doom. He walked up to Josh. "And how do you feel?"

"Hungry," Josh answered.

"I mean, how do you feel that your friend Rodney set off all these explosives in your cabin and that some-one—even you—might have gotten hurt?"

This time Josh gave it some thought. "Still hungry."

I got ready to make a run back into the woods. Todd

was trying to get Josh to attack me. That was his plan!

Todd continued, "Can you believe Rodney would set off fires right next to where you were sleeping? What are you going to do about that?"

"Rodney," Josh barked, "*you* lit that fire?"

"Uhhh," was all I could manage, for even as I tried to think of something to say, Josh was already running at me. I tried to back away, but Magnus seemed to be blocking any escape.

Josh reached me, and I cringed in expectation of the pain. Instead of punching me, though, he put me in a big bear hug. He was going to crush me. What a way to die!

"That was the best, Rodney!" he yelled.

"Huh?" Todd and I said together.

"You knew I love fires! And you made big, banging fires! It's the nicest thing anyone's ever done for me!"

"Ah, well, I thought you'd like it," I said, making sure no one else could hear.

I had never seen Josh so happy. The same couldn't be said for the others—especially Todd, who knew not to push his luck with Josh by my side. I watched as he turned and stormed off with Magnus and the other Algonquins. Mr. Periwinkle shuffled over to us.

"My, my, you two haven't been in camp for one full evening and already all heck's broke loose."

He looked upset and I felt bad for him. "Mr. Periwinkle . . . ," I started to explain.

"It's no good, Rodney. Guess there isn't much use

trying to sleep now. I'll meet you in my office once I get everything here settled."

He walked off into the crowd of campers. So much had happened that I could barely make sense of it all. Josh, on the other hand, had no such problem. He was still grinning away like a kid at a birthday party.

At least someone had enjoyed the first night of camp.